ICE RACE

Published in 2010 by Evans Publishing Ltd,
2A Portman Mansions,
Chiltern St, London WIU 6NR

Reprinted 2011

Editor: Su Swallow
Designer: D.R. Ink

Picture credits:
4: Paul Souders/Corbis. 6: SuperStock/Getty Images. 7: Miha Urbanija./iStock.
8: Richard T. Nowitz/CORBIS. Kenny Viese/iStock.
10-11: Paul Souders/Corbis. 12: Atlantide Phototravel/Corbis.
14: Carl Auer/Corbis. 16: Roman Krochuk/iStock. 18-19: Jeff Vanuga/CORBIS.
20: Paul Souders/Corbis. 22: Shutterstock. 24: Alaska Stock LLC / Alamy.
26: Nathaniel Wilder/Reuters/Corbis. 28: Underwood & Underwood/CORBIS. 30:SuperStock/Getty Images.

British Library Cataloguing in Publication Data

Callery, Sean.

The ice race. -- (Take 2)
1. Dogsledding--Juvenile literature.
I. Title II. Series
798.8'3-dc22

ISBN-13: 9780237542023

Printed by Grafo in Basauri, Spain, February 2011, Job number (CAG1656)

ICE RACE

Sean Callery

Evans

Contents

I am Kody, the lead dog.
I'm excited about the race.

Husky dogs work as a team to pull sleds across the ice and snow of Alaska.

I help my musher pack the sled.

Needed for the race:

Spare boots for each dog

Food

Drink

Sleeping bag

Cooker

Snow shoes

Axe

The musher puts on my booties for me.

The hard, cold ice can damage the dogs' paws, so they wear little boots.

The musher checks the ropes.

The dogs are tied to
the sled so that they
can pull it.

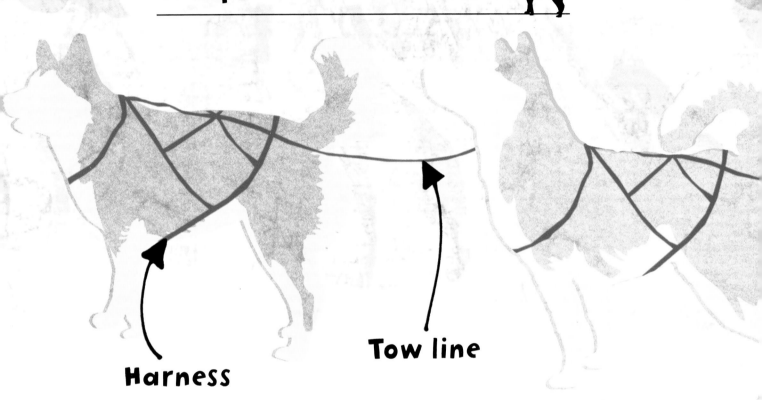

Harness

Tow line

We bark and jump.
We are next!

Each musher pushes his sled to the start line. Sleds set off every two minutes.

I lead the team as we build up speed and pull the sled faster and faster.

Plastic runners

Sleds travel at about 32 kilometres an hour (20 miles per hour). The sled slides across the snow and ice on plastic runners.

This steep hill is hard work!

The Arctic is not all flat. The musher must get off and push the sled up steep hills.

We stop to rest overnight.
There is still a long way to go.

The Iditarod is a famous dog sled race. Teams race more than 1600 kilometres (1000 miles) across Alaska. The fastest sleds finish in eight days.

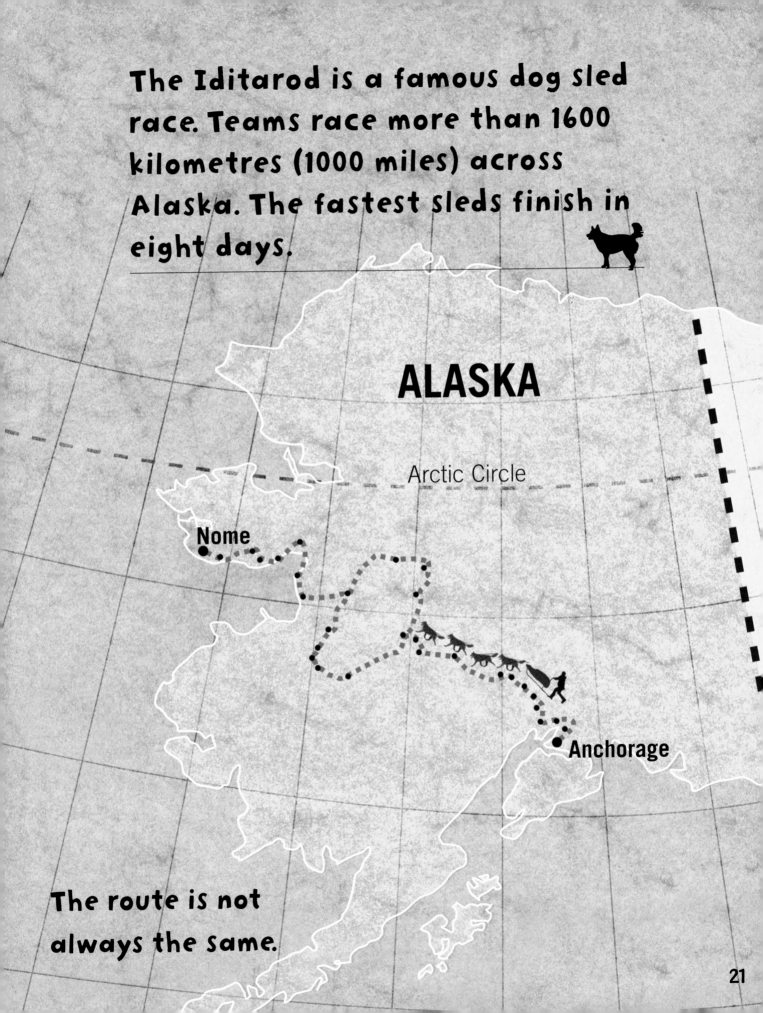

ALASKA

Arctic Circle

Nome

Anchorage

The route is not always the same.

My musher tells us to turn.

Here are some of the words mushers call.

We need to sleep again. It is hard to
stop the sled in snow. The musher uses
a snow hook.

The musher slows the dogs down and throws out the snow hook. It grips in the snow and pulls the sled to stop it.

The finish

That was such fun!
We got a prize!

The first finisher wins money.

The last sled to cross the finish line gets a red lantern. This prize is to show they kept trying to the end.

In 1925, this musher and his dog took part in a race to help some children.

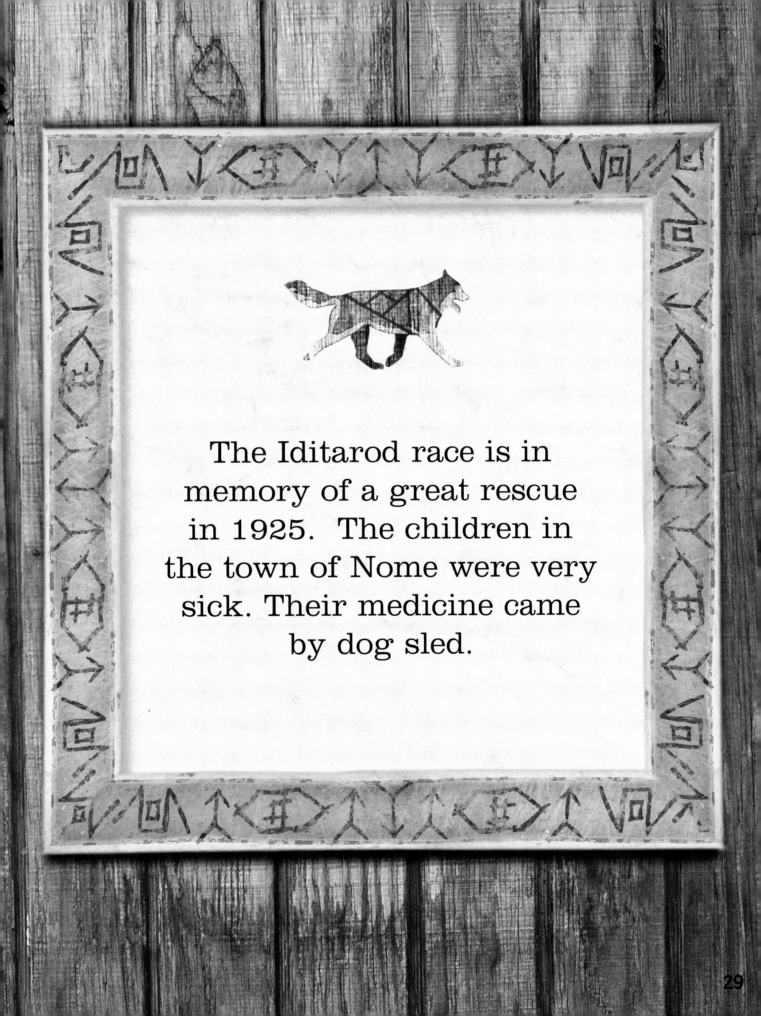

The Iditarod race is in memory of a great rescue in 1925. The children in the town of Nome were very sick. Their medicine came by dog sled.

Glossary

Arctic: icy area around the North Pole.
Husky: special type of dog used to pull a sled.
Musher: the person driving a dog sled.
Runner: the rails on which a sled sits.
Snow shoes: special wide shoes for walking in snow.

Webography

http://www.iditarod.com/
Find out all about the Iditarod race at this site, which includes photographs, videos and a list of mushing words.

http://www.gomush.com/
This website includes coverage of the Iditarod race and its history, with photos, videos and profiles of the mushers.

http://nsidc.org/frozenground/
This website describes what it's like to live on frozen ground and how an icy environment affects plants and animals.

http://www.everythinghusky.com/
A website offering plenty of pictures and information on huskies and mushing, including links to other sites.

Index

If you enjoyed this book, look out for another Take 2 title:

the story of a young boy's fishing trip in the frozen Arctic that did not turn out quite as he had planned.